# the next generation

# the neXt generation

by James Preller

**SCHOLASTIC INC.**

New York    Toronto    London    Auckland    Sydney

**To Nicholas,**
dinosaur lover, meat eater, and future Raptor
—J.P.

**Photo Credits**
**Cover (Bryant), 25 (small):** NBA/Andy Hayt. **Cover (Stoudamire/Iverson), 8, 10, 11, 14 (small), 15 (big), 16 (small), 19 (small), 20 (small), 27 (small), 28 (big), 29 (big):** NBA/Nathaniel S. Butler. **Cover (Garnett), 18 (big), 24 (big):** NBA/Bill Baptist. **Cover (Kidd), 24 (small), 26 (both):** NBA/Sam Forencich. **Cover (Smith), 22 (big):** NBA/Ray Amati. **4, 23 (small):** NBA/Layne Murdoch. **5, 14 (big), 16 (big):** NBA/Andrew D. Bernstein. **6:** NBA/Garett Ellwood. **7, 25 (big):** NBA/Scott Cunningham. **9:** NBA/Dick Raphael. **12 (big):** NBA/Dave Sherman. **12 (small):** NBA/Christopher J. Relke. **13 (big):** NBA/Ronald C. Modra. **13 (small):** NBA/Gary Dineen. **15 (small), 27 (big):** NBA/Louis Capozzola. **17 (both), 29 (small), 31 (big):** NBA/Glenn James. **18 (small):** NBA/Jeff Reinking. **19 (big), 31 (small):** NBA/Fernando Medina. **20 (big):** NBA/Jon Soohoo. **21 (both), 30 (big):** NBA/Barry Gossage. **22 (small):** NBA/Steve Woltman. **23 (big), 28 (small):** NBA/Noren Trotman. **30 (small):** NBA/Steve DiPaola.

If you purchased this book without a cover, you should be aware that this book is stolen property. It was reported as "unsold and destroyed" to the publisher, and neither the author nor the publisher has received payment for this "stripped book."

No part of this publication may be reproduced in whole or in part, or stored in a retrieval system, or transmitted in any form or by any means, electronic, mechanical, photocopying, recording, or otherwise, without written permission of the publisher. For information regarding permission, write to Scholastic Inc., 555 Broadway, New York, NY 10012.

The NBA and individual NBA member team identifications are trademarks, copyrighted designs and other forms of intellectual property of NBA Properties, Inc. and the respective member teams and may not be used without the prior written consent of NBA Properties, Inc. All rights reserved.

ISBN 0-590-37240-8

© 1998 by NBA Properties, Inc.
All rights reserved. Published by Scholastic Inc.

12 11 10 9 8 7 6 5 4 3 2 1                                          8 9/9 0 1 2 3/0

Printed in the U.S.A.
First Scholastic printing, February 1998
Book design: Michael Malone

# It is halftime at the 1997 NBA All-Star Game and a simple but moving ceremony is taking place.

THE ANNOUNCER READS THROUGH A LIST OF 50 NAMES—

BEGINNING WITH MICHAEL JORDAN AND ENDING WITH GEORGE

MIKAN, PROFESSIONAL BASKETBALL'S FIRST TRUE SUPERSTAR.

ONE BY ONE, EACH MAN TAKES HIS PLACE ON THE COURT.

THE LEGENDS GATHER

NO BLARING MUSIC. NO LASERS BOUNCING OFF THE WALLS.

JUST THE QUIET DIGNITY OF BASKETBALL'S GREATEST LEGENDS

GATHERED IN ONE PLACE, STANDING TALL.

## the next generation

ACCORDING TO A PANEL OF EXPERTS, THESE 50 MEN WERE THE BEST THE GAME HAD EVER SEEN (ACTUALLY, 47 MEN—JERRY WEST AND SHAQUILLE O'NEAL WERE UNABLE TO ATTEND AND, SADLY, "PISTOL" PETE MARAVICH PASSED AWAY IN 1988). THE FANS AT GUND ARENA STOOD AND CHEERED. AND FOR MOST, CHERISHED MEMORIES CAME FLASHING BACK: BOB COUSY EXPERTLY LEADING A TWO-ON-ONE BREAK, WILT CHAMBERLAIN THROWING DOWN A THUNDEROUS DUNK, WILLIS REED HOBBLING ONTO THE COURT—SENDING THE MADISON SQUARE GARDEN CROWD INTO A FRENZY—FOR THE DECISIVE GAME IN THE 1970 NBA CHAMPIONSHIP.

ON THIS DAY—FEBRUARY 9, 1997—THE NBA CELEBRATED ITS HISTORY BY HONORING THE PAST. BUT THE FUTURE BELONGS TO A NEW GENERATION OF PLAYERS. FOR ON THAT SAME WEEKEND, A TALENTED GROUP OF YOUNG PLAYERS TOOK THE FLOOR FOR THE ANNUAL SCHICK NBA ROOKIE GAME. FANS WATCHED AS THIS ROOKIE CROP PERFORMED WITH STARTLING ATHLETICISM AND ENERGY, PLAYING THE FAST-PACED, RUN-AND-GUN STYLE THAT SO TYPIFIES TODAY'S YOUNG HOOP STARS.

EIGHTEEN-YEAR-OLD KOBE BRYANT, GIVEN FREE REIGN, POURED IN A RECORD-BREAKING 31 POINTS IN ONLY 26 MINUTES. ANTOINE WALKER SNARED 9 BOARDS IN 23 MINUTES, WHILE MARCUS CAMBY SCORED 18 POINTS AND GRABBED 12 BOARDS IN ONLY 21 MINUTES OF PLAY. ALLEN IVERSON WAS NAMED THE GAME'S MVP FOR BRILLIANTLY ORCHESTRATING THE EASTERN CONFERENCE VICTORY. FOR THE FANS, IT WAS LIKE LOOKING INTO A CRYSTAL BALL AND SEEING THE FUTURE OF NBA BASKETBALL.

KOBE BRYANT

YOUTH WAS ALSO SERVED DURING THE ALL-STAR GAME. ALONGSIDE VETERANS SUCH AS HAKEEM OLAJUWON, SCOTTIE PIPPEN AND PATRICK EWING, THE NBA'S NEXT GENERATION WAS REPRESENTED BY KEVIN GARNETT AND CHRIS WEBBER, EACH MAKING HIS FIRST (BUT SURELY NOT LAST) ALL-STAR APPEARANCE.

# the next generation

## WHO'S NEXT?

THE QUESTION REMAINS: WHO MIGHT BE STANDING, CENTER COURT, WHEN THE NBA CELEBRATES ITS 75TH ANNIVERSARY? WHO ARE THE RISING STARS OF TODAY WHO WILL BE CONSIDERED AMONG THE LEGENDS OF THE GAME? STEPHON MARBURY? CHRIS WEBBER? JASON KIDD? WHO ARE THE BEST YOUNG PLAYERS IN THE GAME?

KEVIN GARNETT

IN *THE NEXT GENERATION* WE'VE PUT THE SPOTLIGHT ON 20 INDIVIDUALS WHO JUST MAY—OVER THE LONG HAUL—TURN INTO LEGENDS. AS A FAN, THAT'S A THRILLING PROSPECT: THE OPPORTUNITY TO WATCH GREATNESS MATURE AND DEVELOP BEFORE OUR EYES. IT'S TOO LATE FOR US TO MARVEL AT A YOUNG ELGIN BAYLOR...OR SEE KAREEM ABDUL-JABBAR ENTER THE LEAGUE AND FLAT-OUT DOMINATE...OR WATCH MAGIC JOHNSON REVOLUTIONIZE THE POINT GUARD POSITION.

BUT WE CAN ENJOY ANTOINE WALKER, KERRY KITTLES AND KOBE BRYANT. CONSIDER KEVIN GARNETT OF THE MINNESOTA TIMBERWOLVES. HE CAME INTO THE LEAGUE AS A SKINNY, 19-YEAR-OLD, 6-10 SMALL FORWARD AND PROMPTLY GREW TWO MORE INCHES IN A YEAR! NOW KEVIN STILL PLAYS THE SO-CALLED *SMALL* FORWARD POSITION, BUT HE BRINGS A WHOLE NEW COMBINATION OF SKILLS TO THE FLOOR. HE'S A BIG MAN WHO CAN HIT THE MID-RANGE JUMPER, PUT THE BALL ON THE FLOOR AND LEAVE A DEFENDER BEHIND WITH A NIFTY CROSSOVER DRIBBLE AND QUICK STEP TO THE HOLE. HE CAN PLAY THE TYPICAL ROLE OF A BIG MAN—BLOCK SHOTS, PULL DOWN REBOUNDS, POST UP ON OFFENSE, *AND* DEFEND THE PERIMETER, *AND* RUN THE FAST BREAK. IN TRUTH, THE NBA HAS NEVER SEEN A PACKAGE QUITE LIKE MR. GARNETT'S. SINGLE-HANDEDLY, HE WILL HELP PULL THE LEAGUE INTO A NEW ERA, AS OPPOSING TEAMS MUST FIND WAYS—*NEW WAYS*—OF STOPPING HIM.

## the next generation

THE COMMON CHARACTERISTICS OF EACH POSITION—POINT GUARD, SHOOTING GUARD, CENTER, POWER FORWARD, SMALL FORWARD—ARE BEING REDEFINED. LOOK AT GRANT HILL, WHO HANDLES THE BALL SO MUCH FOR THE PISTONS THAT HE PLAYS MORE OF A POINT-FORWARD POSITION. SOMETIMES A PLAYER'S TALENT IS SO BIG, SO OUTSIZED, NO TRADITIONAL ROLE CAN CONTAIN HIM. IN THE END, THE NBA IS A PLAYER'S LEAGUE—REINVENTED BY THE GIFTED INDIVIDUALS WHO PLAY IT. SOMETIMES IT'S AS SIMPLE AS ROLLING OUT THE BALL AND WATCHING THESE YOUNG MEN LET IT ALL HANG OUT.

### WHO ARE THE GREATEST?

BILL RUSSELL

PERHAPS THE SUREST MEASURE OF A PLAYER'S GREATNESS IS A QUICK GLANCE AT HIS FINGERS. ARE THERE ANY CHAMPIONSHIP RINGS? BILL RUSSELL EARNED ELEVEN. MAGIC JOHNSON HAS FIVE. LARRY BIRD, THREE. CRITICS ONCE WHISPERED THAT MICHAEL JORDAN WASN'T TRULY GREAT BECAUSE DURING HIS FIRST SIX YEARS IN THE LEAGUE HE HADN'T BEEN ABLE TO LEAD THE CHICAGO BULLS TO AN NBA CHAMPIONSHIP. WELL, NEEDLESS TO SAY, THOSE CRITICS HAVE BEEN SILENCED FOREVER. OF COURSE, IT MUST BE SAID THAT THIS PARTICULAR MEASUREMENT CAN BE A LITTLE UNFAIR TO ALL THE GREAT PLAYERS WHO SUFFERED ON SOME NOT-SO-GREAT TEAMS. YOU CAN'T WIN A CHAMPIONSHIP BY YOURSELF, BUT THE BASIC QUESTION STANDS: IS HE A WINNER?

THAT WILL BE THE ULTIMATE TEST FOR THE PLAYERS FEATURED IN THIS BOOK. FOR MOST OF THEM, THE JURY IS STILL OUT. FEW CAN REASONABLY DOUBT THEIR INDIVIDUAL ABILITIES. BUT ARE THEY WINNERS? ARE THEY WILLING TO MAKE INDIVIDUAL SACRIFICES FOR THE GOOD OF THE TEAM? THE BEST PLAYERS DO.

# the next generation

## FLASH BACK, FAST FORWARD

FLASH BACK TO 1986, WHEN THE LEADER OF THAT PERIOD'S "NEXT GENERATION" WAS A FLASHY SCORER NAMED MICHAEL JORDAN. HE'D ALREADY WON NBA ROOKIE OF THE YEAR THE PREVIOUS SEASON, AVERAGING A REMARKABLE 28.2 POINTS A GAME. BUT DESPITE JORDAN'S INDIVIDUAL HEROICS, THE BULLS WERE STILL A LOSING TEAM WITH A 38-44 RECORD. THE NEXT SEASON, 1985-86, THINGS ONLY GOT WORSE AS JORDAN WAS INJURED FOR ALL BUT 18 REGULAR-SEASON GAMES. YET MICHAEL MADE IT BACK FOR THE PLAYOFFS—AND MAN, DID HE PUT ON A SHOW.

ON APRIL 20, 1986, THE UNDERDOG BULLS WENT UP AGAINST LARRY BIRD AND THE BOSTON CELTICS. IN GAME 2 OF THAT FIRST-ROUND SERIES, A BACK-AND-FORTH STRUGGLE THAT WENT INTO DOUBLE OVERTIME, MICHAEL POURED IN A RECORD-BREAKING 63 POINTS. STILL, THE BULLS LOST THE GAME AND THE SERIES, THREE GAMES TO NONE. JORDAN COMMENTED AFTER THE GAME, "FORGET THE RECORD, I'D GIVE ALL THE POINTS BACK IF WE COULD WIN."

MICHAEL KNEW THAT WINNING WAS THE ONLY GOAL, THE TRUEST MEASURE OF GREATNESS. INDIVIDUAL SUCCESS WAS NICE, BUT AT THE END OF THE DAY, LEADING A TEAM TO VICTORY WAS ALL THAT MATTERED.

MICHAEL JORDAN VS. LARRY BIRD, 1986 PLAYOFFS

## the next generation

NOW FAST FORWARD TO A REMARKABLE SERIES OF GAMES PLAYED BY 1997 SCHICK NBA ROOKIE OF THE YEAR, ALLEN IVERSON. IN FIVE CONSECUTIVE GAMES, ALLEN LIT UP THE SCOREBOARD, AVERAGING 43.6 POINTS A GAME. HIS PERFORMANCE WAS TRULY ASTONISHING, THE LONGEST HIGH-SCORING STREAK BY A ROOKIE IN LEAGUE HISTORY. IN TRUTH, THE NBA HADN'T SEEN A ROOKIE PERFORM AT THIS LEVEL SINCE, WELL, MICHAEL JORDAN. BUT NOTE THIS: IVERSON'S TEAM, THE PHILADELPHIA 76ERS, LOST EVERY ONE OF THE FIVE GAMES. DOES THAT MAKE MR. IVERSON A BAD PLAYER? HARDLY. IT ONLY SERVES TO POINT OUT THAT FOR IVERSON TO BE CONSIDERED TRULY GREAT—ON A PAR WITH LEGENDS LIKE RUSSELL, BIRD, JOHNSON AND JORDAN—HE'LL NEED TO DO MORE THAN FATTEN INDIVIDUAL STATISTICS. HE'LL NEED TO WIN, AND WIN OFTEN.

ALLEN IVERSON

THE SAME IS TRUE FOR EVERY PLAYER IN THE BOOK. OF COURSE, NO ONE MAN CAN CARRY A TEAM FOR LONG STRETCHES OF TIME. EVEN MICHAEL JORDAN COULDN'T WIN IN CHICAGO UNTIL HE WAS SURROUNDED BY THE RIGHT COMPLEMENTARY PLAYERS. BUT REGARDLESS OF HOW WELL EACH OF THE PLAYERS IN THIS BOOK FARES OVER TIME, ONE THING IS SURE. THE NBA NOW FEATURES A GREAT NEW INFLUX OF TALENT—PLAYERS WITH ASTONISHING ATHLETICISM AND JAW-DROPPING SKILLS.

SO SIT BACK AND ENJOY THE SHOW.

## A FEW SIMPLE GUIDELINES

Our list of 20 players is in no way an "official" list. We did it for fun, for entertainment, and perhaps to start a few friendly arguments. Next year, surely, the list will change, as new athletes filter into the NBA and a few high-flying hopefuls come back to earth. We came up with some guidelines that helped us answer the basic question, *Who are the best young players in the NBA?*

1) Each player must have played in the NBA during the 1996-97 season with one notable exception: Mr. Tim Duncan, the first player selected in the 1997 NBA Draft. No disrespect to promising prospects such as Keith Van Horn and Ray Mercer, but Duncan is in a category of his own. As the No. 1 selection in the draft, we felt he deserved special recognition.

2) Each player must be younger than 25 years old at the publication date of this book, February 1, 1998. Juwan Howard, with a birthdate of February 7, 1973, was the oldest player to make the cut. Grant Hill, perhaps the finest representative of the NBA's next generation, isn't included because he's a few months too old.

3) We limited the number of players to 20 for an arbitrary reason. We thought the idea of "20 Under 25" just sounded kind of cool. Also, players tend to hit their prime during the ages of 26 to 29. In this way, it's safe to assume that for every player in this book, the best is yet to come.

MARCUS CAMBY

BORN: 12/11/76 • HEIGHT: 6-9 • COLLEGE: CALIFORNIA • DRAFTED: #3, 1996

The third player selected in the 1996 NBA Draft—surely one of the richest, deepest talent pools in recent history—small forward Abdur-Rahim possesses all the tools to become an explosive talent in the NBA. Significantly, "Reef" got better as the season wore on, averaging 21.3 points and 7.9 rebounds per game after the All-Star break. A devout Muslim, Abdur-Rahim is polite, unselfish and a tireless worker. He was twice named "Mr. Basketball" in Georgia, averaging 31 points and 12 rebounds as a high school senior. Reef capped off the season by being named to the 1996-97 NBA All-Rookie First Team, the only unanimous selection in the group.

# Shareef Abdur-Rahim

### CAREER HIGHS

**37 Points** vs. Sacramento 1/11/97

**17 Rebounds** vs. Dallas 4/12/97

**10 Assists** vs. Phoenix 4/19/97

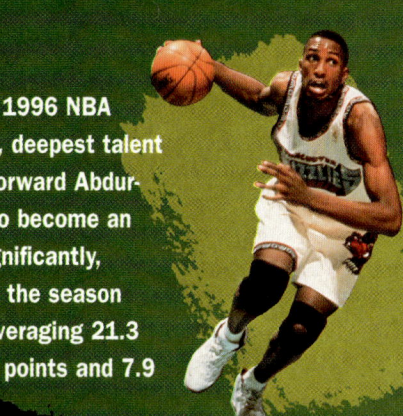

BORN: 7/20/75 • HEIGHT: 6-5 • COLLEGE: CONNECTICUT • DRAFTED: #5, 1996

# Ray Allen

### CAREER HIGHS

32 Points vs. Phoenix 3/25/97

9 Rebounds (two times)

9 Assists vs. Philadelphia 2/1/97

Putting together an NBA franchise is a lot like constructing a jigsaw puzzle. First you need the pieces. The Bucks were solid up front with Glenn "Big Dog" Robinson and Vin Baker, but undermanned in the backcourt. Enter Ray Allen, who immediately gave the rugged Bucks an outside game. He rebounds, passes, takes his man off the dribble, and can spot up for the three. During a distinguished college career at the University of Connecticut (where he played alongside fellow NBAer Travis Knight), Ray's consistent, all-around effort earned him All-America recognition in back-to-back seasons. Ray is also an all-around good guy: His Ray of Hope Foundation provides food and clothing for the needy.

13

# Kobe Bryant

**1997 NESTLÉ CRUNCH SLAM DUNK CHAMPION**

BORN: 8/23/78 • HEIGHT: 6-6

HIGH SCHOOL: LOWER MERION (PA) • DRAFTED: #13, 1996

## CAREER HIGHS

**24 Points** vs. Golden State 4/18/97

**8 Rebounds** vs. Vancouver 3/27/97

**5 Assists** vs. Detroit 1/18/97

Two words: Kobe can. And *Kobe will*. Clearly, Kobe has the moves and the moxie to become an impact player in the NBA. Kobe made his professional debut just two months and eleven days after his 18th birthday, making him the youngest player ever to appear in an NBA game. Now it's just a matter of getting the experience to catch up with all that eye-popping talent.

Playing an average of only 15.5 minutes a game for the talent-rich Lakers, Kobe still managed to showcase his considerable skills. If it seems like Kobe was born to be a star, it might be in his genes. Kobe's father was Joe "Jelly Bean" Bryant, an eight-year NBA veteran with the Philadelphia 76ers, San Diego Clippers and Houston Rockets.

14

BORN: 3/22/74 • HEIGHT: 6-11 • COLLEGE: MASSACHUSETTS • DRAFTED: #2, 1996

# Marcus Camby

"Any big man would love to play with Damon," Marcus Camby said, moments after being selected by the Toronto Raptors in the 1996 NBA Draft. It was a joyous day for the Raptors, for in consecutive drafts they had acquired two building blocks for the future: First, a pint-sized speedster at the point in Damon Stoudamire, then a mobile shotblocker by the name of Camby. Marcus brings to the Raptors the low-post scoring threat they needed. He features magical moves and a deft shooting touch. He can hit the mid-range jumper, as well as face the basket and make graceful, slashing drives to the hoop. Marcus concluded the season by placing 10th in blocks per game and was named to the 1996-97 NBA All-Rookie First Team.

## CAREER HIGHS

37 Points vs. Atlanta 3/23/97

16 Rebounds vs. Charlotte 3/21/97

9 Blocks vs. Phoenix 2/1/97

BORN: 4/25/76 • HEIGHT: 6-10 • COLLEGE: WAKE FOREST • DRAFTED: #1, 1997

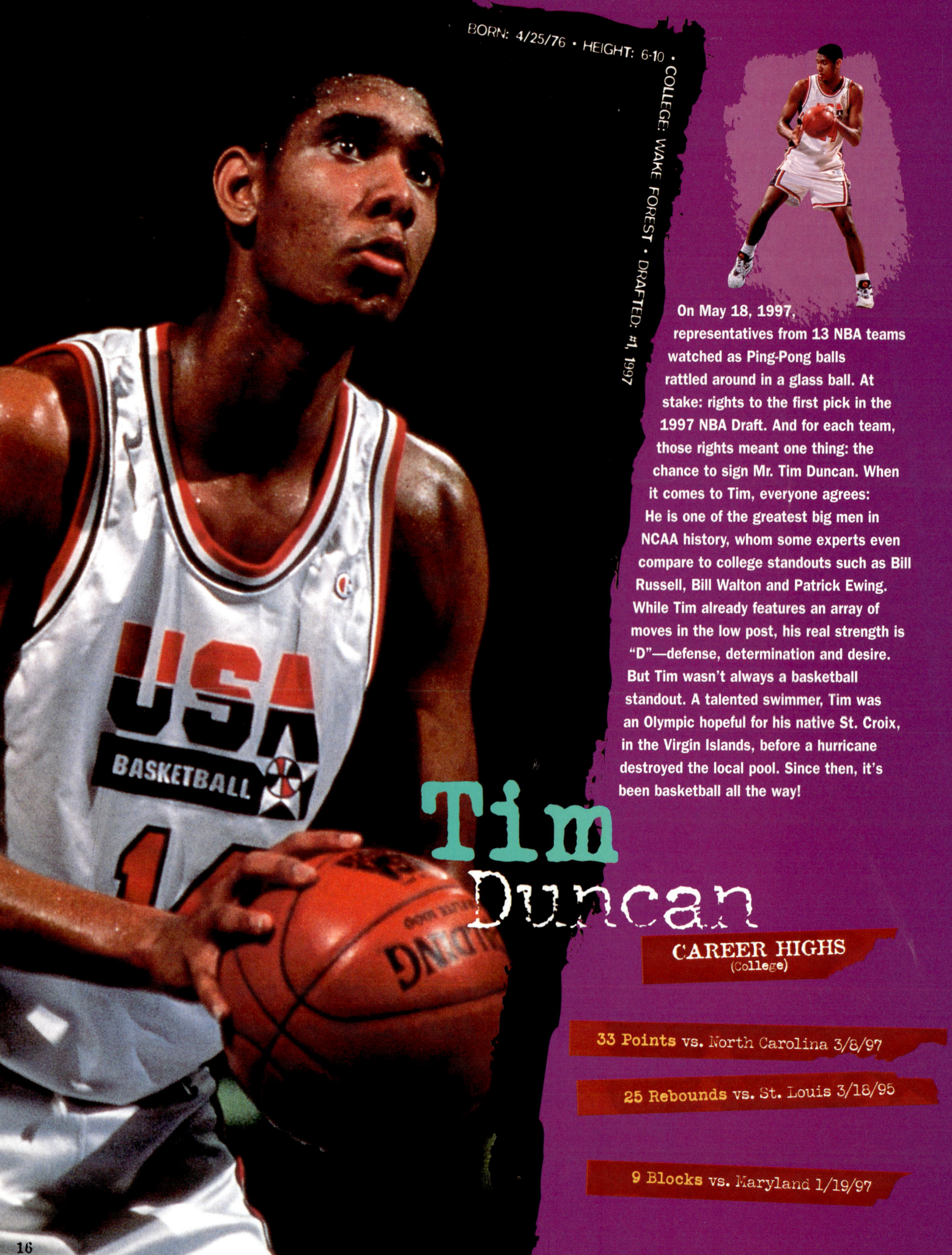

On May 18, 1997, representatives from 13 NBA teams watched as Ping-Pong balls rattled around in a glass ball. At stake: rights to the first pick in the 1997 NBA Draft. And for each team, those rights meant one thing: the chance to sign Mr. Tim Duncan. When it comes to Tim, everyone agrees: He is one of the greatest big men in NCAA history, whom some experts even compare to college standouts such as Bill Russell, Bill Walton and Patrick Ewing. While Tim already features an array of moves in the low post, his real strength is "D"—defense, determination and desire. But Tim wasn't always a basketball standout. A talented swimmer, Tim was an Olympic hopeful for his native St. Croix, in the Virgin Islands, before a hurricane destroyed the local pool. Since then, it's been basketball all the way!

# Tim Duncan

## CAREER HIGHS
(College)

33 Points vs. North Carolina 3/8/97

25 Rebounds vs. St. Louis 3/18/95

9 Blocks vs. Maryland 1/19/97

# Michael Finley

BORN: 3/6/73 • HEIGHT: 6-7 • COLLEGE: WISCONSIN • DRAFTED: #21, 1995

### CAREER HIGHS

**33 Points** vs. Milwaukee 2/20/97

**10 Rebounds** (five times)

**10 Assists** vs. Dallas 1/12/96

Every draft has one or two—the quality player who, for whatever reason, eludes the spotlight. So it was with Michael Finley, one of the surprises of the 1995 rookie class. On draft day, Michael's name wasn't called until the Phoenix Suns made him the 21st overall selection. But talent and desire have a way of rising to the top. By the end of the year, Michael was named to the 1995-96 NBA All-Rookie First Team. After all, Michael's rookie effort was too good to be ignored. He played in all 82 games, was runner-up to Brent Barry in the Nestlé Crunch Slam Dunk contest, and averaged 15.0 points per game. Acquired by Dallas in the Jason Kidd trade, Michael thrives in a fast-paced, open-court game, where his soaring athleticism gives him the freedom to create.

17

BORN: 5/19/76 • HEIGHT: 7-0 • HIGH SCHOOL: FARRAGUT ACADEMY (IL) • DRAFTED: #5, 1995

# Kevin Garnett

At the end of his second NBA season, Kevin Garnett and the Minnesota Timberwolves found themselves in an unfamiliar place—the NBA Playoffs. The young T-Wolves went up against the Houston Rockets, a team with Hakeem Olajuwon, Clyde Drexler and Charles Barkley—three of the 50 Greatest Players in NBA history. It was a fascinating matchup, watching the youngsters battle the savvy veterans, as if a torch were about to be passed. But the playoff-tough Rockets weren't quite ready to surrender the flame. Though Kevin battled valiantly, at times making plays that had even Barkley shaking his head in wonder, the T-Wolves were swept in three. File it under: *Lessons Learned*. Now look for the student to become the master.

## CAREER HIGHS

33 Points (two times)

19 Rebounds vs. Philadelphia 3/6/96

8 Blocks (two times)

## CAREER HIGHS

42 Points vs. Toronto 4/19/96

15 Rebounds (two times)

9 Assists (five times)

# Juwan Howard

BORN: 2/7/73 • HEIGHT: 6-9 • COLLEGE: MICHIGAN • DRAFTED: #5, 1994

During his college career at Michigan, Juwan was part of a great freshman class that came to be known as "The Fab Five." His teammates included Chris Webber and Jalen Rose, both of whom became first-round picks in the NBA Draft. During the 1995-96 season, Juwan—by then an All-Star for the Washington Bullets (now named the Wizards)—was joined by his old friend Chris Webber. They've been making sweet music ever since, leading the young, up-and-coming team to the NBA Playoffs for the first time in nine long years. Unlike some of his young peers, Juwan is a quiet star. Without a lot of flash and fury, Juwan is a silent assassin—in a calm, professional manner, he simply goes about the job of beating opponents.

When asked who in the NBA could guard him one-on-one, Allen Iverson responded matter-of-factly, "Nobody." *No-bah-dee*. Allen takes that same confidence onto the court—he's absolutely fearless and doesn't back down from anyone. Allen shows his respect for the game—and for those who play it—by giving everything he's got night in, night out. As a rookie, Allen's electrifying play turned heads all season long (mostly hapless defenders watching him whiz past), culminating with a 23.5 points-per-game average (sixth in the NBA) and the Schick NBA Rookie of the Year Award. Faster than a speeding bullet, able to leap over taller defenders in a single bound, Allen Iverson just may be the NBA's next Superman.

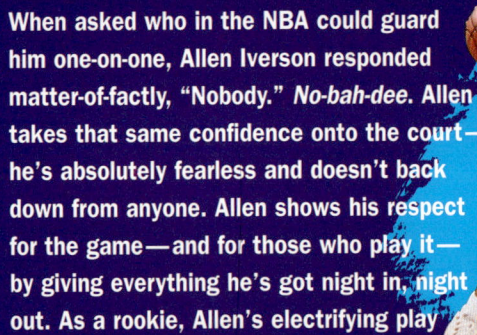

# Allen Iverson

**1997 SCHICK NBA ROOKIE OF THE YEAR**

### CAREER HIGHS

50 Points vs. Cleveland 4/12/97

15 Assists vs. Boston 4/18/97

6 Steals vs. Vancouver 11/30/96

BORN: 6/7/75 • HEIGHT: 6-0 • COLLEGE: GEORGETOWN • DRAFTED: #1, 1996

BORN: 3/23/73 • HEIGHT: 6-4 • COLLEGE: CALIFORNIA • DRAFTED: #2, 1994

# Jason Kidd

**1995 SCHICK NBA CO-ROOKIE OF THE YEAR**

In his rookie season, Jason Kidd set the NBA on fire with his genius for making the right pass...to the right person... at the right time. As pure a playmaker as the league has ever seen, the sturdy point guard took the Dallas Mavericks from 13 to 36 wins and tied Grant Hill for Rookie of the Year honors. In his second season, Jason improved significantly in assists, rebounds and points per game. As a result, he became the first Dallas Maverick to start an All-Star Game. But after struggling early in his third NBA season, Jason was shipped to the Phoenix Suns in a trade that shocked most NBA observers. Now Jason brings his creative, entertaining, up-tempo style of play to Phoenix— where the future suddenly looks a whole lot brighter.

## CAREER HIGHS

38 Points vs. Houston 4/11/95

16 Rebounds vs. L.A. Clippers 1/30/96

25 Assists vs. Utah 2/8/96

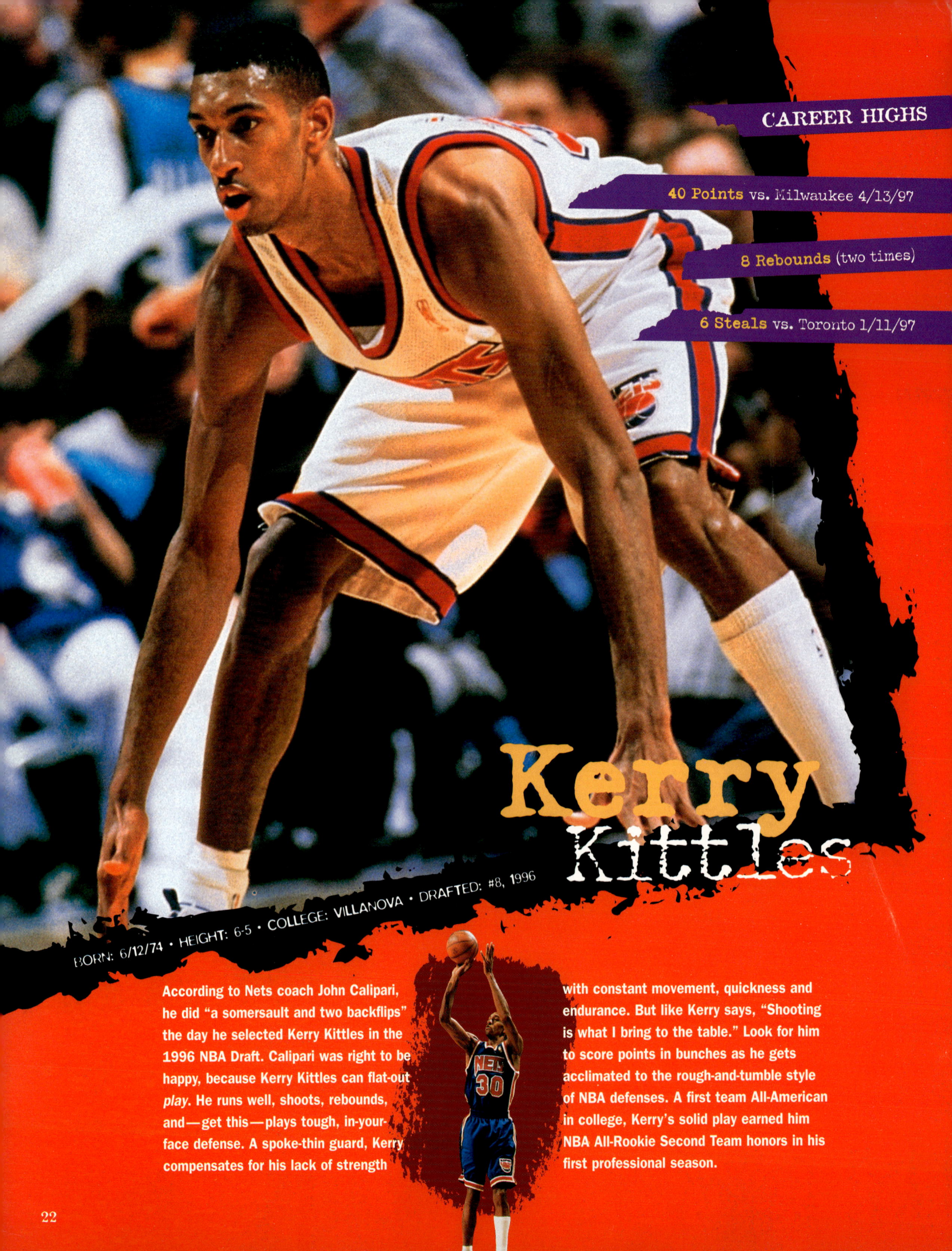

## CAREER HIGHS

40 Points vs. Milwaukee 4/13/97

8 Rebounds (two times)

6 Steals vs. Toronto 1/11/97

# Kerry Kittles

BORN: 6/12/74 • HEIGHT: 6-5 • COLLEGE: VILLANOVA • DRAFTED: #8, 1996

According to Nets coach John Calipari, he did "a somersault and two backflips" the day he selected Kerry Kittles in the 1996 NBA Draft. Calipari was right to be happy, because Kerry Kittles can flat-out *play*. He runs well, shoots, rebounds, and—get this—plays tough, in-your-face defense. A spoke-thin guard, Kerry compensates for his lack of strength with constant movement, quickness and endurance. But like Kerry says, "Shooting is what I bring to the table." Look for him to score points in bunches as he gets acclimated to the rough-and-tumble style of NBA defenses. A first team All-American in college, Kerry's solid play earned him NBA All-Rookie Second Team honors in his first professional season.

BORN: 2/20/77 • HEIGHT: 6-2 • COLLEGE: GEORGIA TECH • DRAFTED: #4, 1996

# Stephon Marbury

Sure, the Minnesota Timberwolves were turning things around even before Mr. "Starbury" entered the picture. With Tom Gugliotta and Kevin Garnett up front, the T-Wolves were young and gifted. But it took Stephon's arrival—and pure point guard skills—to turn the once-toothless T-Wolves into a team. Thing is, Stephon's game is pure wonder. He'll whip a behind-the-back pass, skip past a defender with a leave-your-shoes-in-concrete crossover dribble, slam an alley-oop and nail a big three. Importantly, Stephon showed true grit in the playoffs, driving, spinning and shooting for 28 points in Game 1 against the Rockets. Stephon placed a close second behind Allen Iverson for Schick NBA Rookie of the Year. And he just turned twenty-one.

### CAREER HIGHS

33 Points vs. Utah 12/23/96

7 Rebounds (four times)

17 Assists vs. Milwaukee 4/18/97

23

DRAFTED: #2, 1995 • COLLEGE: ALABAMA • HEIGHT: 6-9 • BORN: 9/7/74

# Antonio McDyess

Nope, it's not a bird. And it's not a plane. It's just Antonio McDyess doing his thing. It's appropriate that Antonio McDyess plays his home games in Denver, also known as the Mile High City, because he's been asked to live up to some pretty high expectations. Fortunately, with a 47-inch one-step leap, Antonio regularly reaches incredible heights. Another in the new generation of unusually tall, shotblocking *small* forwards, Antonio was named to the NBA All-Rookie First Team in 1996. His progress continued in his second year with the Nuggets. Not an offensive powerhouse, the Nuggets needed more production from Antonio and he responded, raising his points-per-game average from 13.4 to 18.3. With progress like that, the sky's the limit.

## CAREER HIGHS

35 Points vs. Golden State 4/10/97

18 Rebounds vs. San Antonio 4/8/97

6 Blocks vs. San Antonio 11/3/96

24

Shaquille O'Neal entered the NBA in 1992 and the ripple effect was immediate. Instantly, opposing teams needed players who could put a body on Shaq. So the search was on for big, strong, physical players. Well, that's one problem Vancouver doesn't need to worry about. They've got "Big Country." Bryant Reeves grew up (and up and up) in Gans, Oklahoma, a town so small that it doesn't even have a stoplight. While the NBA was always a dream for Bryant, he claims if it didn't work out he could always become a cattleman. Well, the cows are going to have to wait. Because in only two NBA seasons, Bryant has established himself as a big-time presence in the paint—providing the Grizzlies with muscle, scoring and tough interior defense.

BORN: 6/8/73 • HEIGHT: 7-0 • COLLEGE: OKLAHOMA STATE • DRAFTED: #6, 1995

# Bryant Reeves

## CAREER HIGHS

39 Points vs. Phoenix 4/19/97

18 Rebounds (two times)

7 Blocks vs. Sacramento 4/12/96

BORN: 7/26/75 • HEIGHT: 6-10 • COLLEGE: MARYLAND • DRAFTED: #1, 1995

Joe Smith grew up idolizing Magic Johnson. That's why the slender forward wears No. 32 on his jersey—it was Magic's number. There's another connection: Only one player in NBA history was selected first overall in the NBA Draft at a younger age than Joe Smith, who entered after his sophomore season. The player? You guessed it—Magic Johnson. Poised and calm, Joe proved his worth immediately, scoring 30 points in just his fourth NBA game. In his second season, Joe averaged a very solid 18.7 points and 8.5 boards. Commented Laker coach Del Harris, "He's so good he stops speeding bullets." Joe's fans can catch him in the movie *Rebound*, in which he portrays NBA great Connie Hawkins.

# Joe Smith

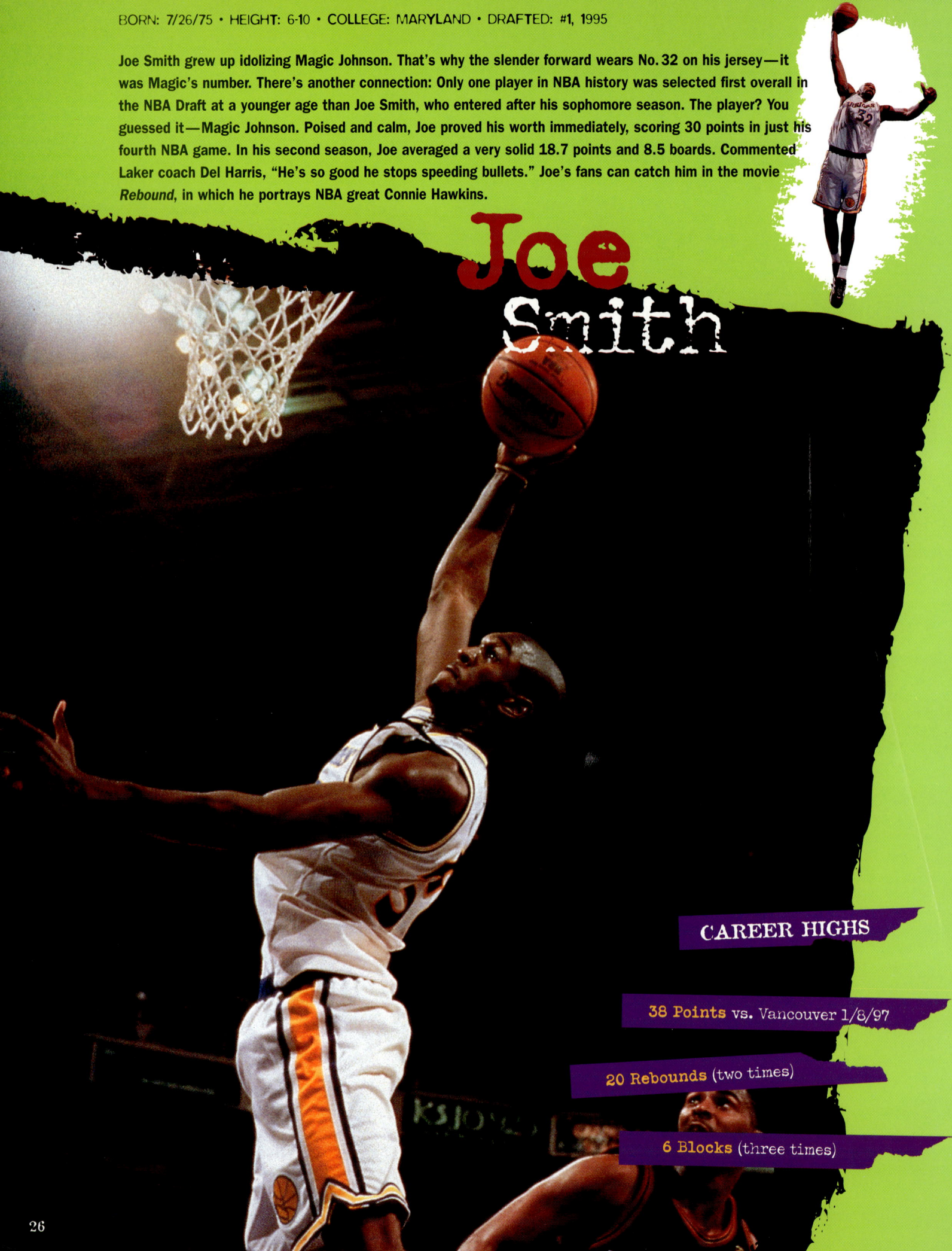

### CAREER HIGHS

38 Points vs. Vancouver 1/8/97

20 Rebounds (two times)

6 Blocks (three times)

BORN: 11/5/74 • HEIGHT: 6-6 • COLLEGE: NORTH CAROLINA • DRAFTED: #3, 1995

# Jerry Stackhouse

## CAREER HIGHS

39 Points vs. Charlotte 4/5/97

15 Rebounds vs. Utah 12/20/95

10 Assists vs. Houston 11/22/95

It's just not fair. Since his early college days, Jerry Stackhouse has been compared to Michael Jordan. And in all honesty, there *are* similarities. Both play the same position—with acrobatic flair and a gift for creating in midair. Jerry, like Michael, starred under Coach Dean Smith at North Carolina. And both are highly competitive—hard workers, driven to succeed. But like Magic Johnson once said, "There's Michael, and then there's everybody else." Jerry has done well to shun the comparisons and let his game do the talking. Spin, pump fake, double clutch, swish. Enough said. Averaging 20.7 points per game for the 1996-97 season, Jerry's game says it all. Let Jordan be Jordan. Jerry's got his own thing and he's only getting better.

BORN: 9/3/73 • HEIGHT: 5-10 • COLLEGE: ARIZONA • DRAFTED: #7, 1995

# Damon Stoudamire

**CAREER HIGHS**

35 Points (two times)

12 Rebounds vs. Seattle 11/21/95

19 Assists vs. Houston 2/27/96

**1996 SCHICK NBA ROOKIE OF THE YEAR**

The fans in Toronto booed when the expansion Raptors selected a virtually unknown point guard, Damon Stoudamire, in the first round of the NBA Draft. Damon's reply? He confidently reasoned, "I knew that once they saw me play, they'd like me." That was no idle boast. Damon was named 1996 Schick NBA Rookie of the Year. And with each dazzling drive to the hole and last-second dish to an open teammate, Damon continues to prove the boo-birds wrong. His speed presents defensive problems for every team, because few players can match him stride-for-stride. Damon concluded his second season by averaging 20.2 points, 8.8 assists and 4.1 rebounds per game—not bad for a guy who is only 5-10!

# Antoine Walker

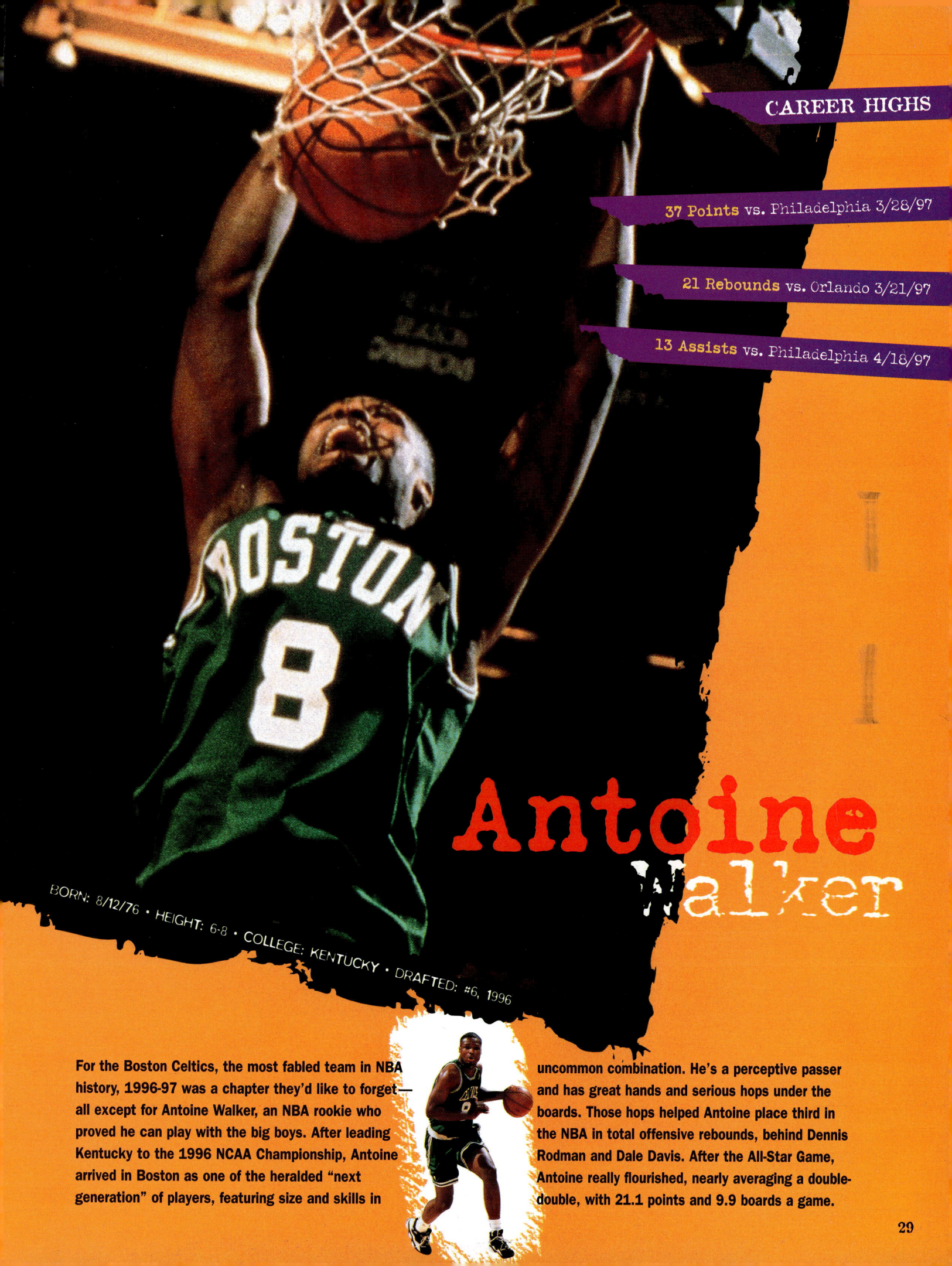

## CAREER HIGHS

**37 Points** vs. Philadelphia 3/28/97

**21 Rebounds** vs. Orlando 3/21/97

**13 Assists** vs. Philadelphia 4/18/97

BORN: 8/12/76 • HEIGHT: 6-8 • COLLEGE: KENTUCKY • DRAFTED: #6, 1996

For the Boston Celtics, the most fabled team in NBA history, 1996-97 was a chapter they'd like to forget—all except for Antoine Walker, an NBA rookie who proved he can play with the big boys. After leading Kentucky to the 1996 NCAA Championship, Antoine arrived in Boston as one of the heralded "next generation" of players, featuring size and skills in uncommon combination. He's a perceptive passer and has great hands and serious hops under the boards. Those hops helped Antoine place third in the NBA in total offensive rebounds, behind Dennis Rodman and Dale Davis. After the All-Star Game, Antoine really flourished, nearly averaging a double-double, with 21.1 points and 9.9 boards a game.

Rasheed Wallace had a good, solid rookie year. Then, after being traded from Washington to Portland in the Rod Strickland deal, he suddenly got a whole lot better—raising his scoring average by five full points. His strong sophomore effort, featuring a tough-as-nails interior game, was recognized when Rasheed was third in voting for the NBA's Most Improved Player (behind Isaac Austin and Doug Christie). That improvement will surely continue, for Rasheed has dominated at every level of play. In high school he was named *USA Today* High School Player of the Year, averaging 16 points, 15 rebounds and 7 blocks despite playing just 19 minutes a game. In college, Rasheed teamed up with Jerry Stackhouse to lead the North Carolina Tar Heels to the 1995 NCAA Final Four.

# Rasheed Wallace

### CAREER HIGHS

38 Points vs. Sacramento 12/21/96

14 Rebounds (two times)

5 Blocks vs. New Jersey 11/28/95

BORN: 9/17/74 • HEIGHT: 6-10 • COLLEGE: NORTH CAROLINA • DRAFTED: #4, 1995

BORN: 3/1/73 • HEIGHT: 6-10 • COLLEGE: MICHIGAN • DRAFTED: #1, 1993

# Chris Webber

**1994 SCHICK NBA ROOKIE OF THE YEAR**

It's hard to think of this four-year veteran—featuring a condorlike 87-inch wingspan—as part of the NBA's next generation of stars. But birth certificates don't lie. Though injuries have slowed Webber's rise to superstardom, it was only a matter of time before this former No. 1 pick took his place among the elite. Chris showed exactly why he deserved the top slot when he became the first rookie in NBA history to total more than 1,000 points, 500 rebounds, 250 assists, 150 blocks and 75 steals. That, folks, indicates an extremely well-rounded game. Of course, anyone who saw him play as a kid could have predicted it: Chris scored 64 points—and slammed home 15 dunks—in one game as an eighth-grader! Chris appeared in his first All-Star Game last season.

### CAREER HIGHS

40 Points vs. Golden State 12/27/95

21 Rebounds (two times)

7 Blocks vs. Seattle 11/20/96

# ODDS & ENDS

## NBA ALL-ROOKIE TEAMS

### 1995
**FIRST TEAM**
**Jason Kidd,** *Dallas*
**Grant Hill,** *Detroit*
**Glenn Robinson,** *Milwaukee*
**Eddie Jones,** *L.A. Lakers*
**Brian Grant,** *Sacramento*

**SECOND TEAM**
**Juwan Howard,** *Washington*
**Eric Montross,** *Boston*
**Wesley Person,** *Phoenix*
**Jalen Rose,** *Denver*
**Donyell Marshall,** *Golden State*
**Sharone Wright,** *Philadelphia*

### 1996
**FIRST TEAM**
**Damon Stoudamire,** *Toronto*
**Joe Smith,** *Golden State*
**Jerry Stackhouse,** *Philadelphia*
**Antonio McDyess,** *Denver*
**Arvydas Sabonis,** *Portland*
**Michael Finley,** *Phoenix*

**SECOND TEAM**
**Kevin Garnett,** *Minnesota*
**Bryant Reeves,** *Vancouver*
**Brent Barry,** *L.A. Clippers*
**Rasheed Wallace,** *Washington*
**Tyus Edney,** *Sacramento*

### 1997
**FIRST TEAM**
**Allen Iverson,** *Philadelphia*
**Stephon Marbury,** *Minnesota*
**Marcus Camby,** *Toronto*
**Shareef Abdur-Rahim,** *Vancouver*
**Antoine Walker,** *Boston*

**SECOND TEAM**
**Kerry Kittles,** *New Jersey*
**Ray Allen,** *Milwaukee*
**Travis Knight,** *L.A. Lakers*
**Kobe Bryant,** *L.A. Lakers*
**Matt Maloney,** *Houston*

## SCHICK NBA ROOKIE OF THE YEAR WINNERS

| | |
|---|---|
| 1984-85 | Michael Jordan, *Chicago* |
| 1985-86 | Patrick Ewing, *New York* |
| 1986-87 | Chuck Person, *Indiana* |
| 1987-88 | Mark Jackson, *New York* |
| 1988-89 | Mitch Richmond, *Golden State* |
| 1989-90 | David Robinson, *San Antonio* |
| 1990-91 | Derrick Coleman, *New Jersey* |
| 1991-92 | Larry Johnson, *Charlotte* |
| 1992-93 | Shaquille O'Neal, *Orlando* |
| 1993-94 | Chris Webber, *Golden State* |
| 1994-95 | Grant Hill, *Detroit* |
| | Jason Kidd, *Dallas* |
| 1995-96 | Damon Stoudamire, *Toronto* |
| 1996-97 | Allen Iverson, *Philadelphia* |

## No. 1 NBA DRAFT PICKS

1984 Hakeem Olajuwon
1985 Patrick Ewing
1986 Brad Daugherty
1987 David Robinson *
1988 Danny Manning
1989 Pervis Ellison
1990 Derrick Coleman
1991 Larry Johnson
1992 Shaquille O'Neal
1993 Chris Webber
1994 Glenn Robinson
1995 Joe Smith
1996 Allen Iverson
1997 Tim Duncan

*\* did not play until 1989-90 season due to military commitments*